THOMAS & FRIENDS

Thomas and the New Carousel

Today is the first day of the Sodor Summer Festival!  Thomas wakes up early because he is very excited.

People from all over the island will come to the festival to listen to music, eat special treats, play games, and go on rides. Thomas has also heard that this year, Sir Topham Hatt is bringing a special ride to the festival—a new carousel!

"I hope Sir Topham Hatt will ask me to pick up the new carousel," Thomas thinks. "Then everyone will know I am a very important engine."

Sir Topham Hatt arrives at Tidmouth Sheds to give the engines their jobs. Rosie will pick up the horses for the horse show.  Percy is to pull the tables and chairs. Emily will pick up passengers from Knapford Station. And Stanley will pull the Ferris wheel.

"What about me?" peeps Thomas.

"Thomas," says Sir Topham Hatt, "I would like you to pick up the new carousel from Brendam Docks."

Thomas is very pleased.

"This is a very important job, Thomas," adds Sir Topham Hatt. "I need you to be very careful."

"I will," promises Thomas.

At the freight yard, Thomas is coupled to two flatbeds. Then he chuffs happily to Brendam Docks.

"Hello, Thomas," says Salty. "What brings you to the docks?"

"Sir Topham Hatt asked me to pick up the new carousel for the summer festival," replies Thomas.

"The festival, the festival," grumbles Cranky. "All anybody talks about is the festival." Cranky lowers four big crates onto the two flatbeds.

"I can't wait to show everyone how important I am," peeps Thomas. He is so excited that he pulls away before the workers have fastened all the crates!

Thomas puffs all over the Island of Sodor so everybody can see what an important engine he is.

He chuffs through the countryside and whooshes past the quarry.

He flies through tunnels and crosses a large bridge.

Wherever he goes, he peeps his whistle loudly so everyone will notice him. Today Thomas feels very important indeed.

Finally, Thomas decides it is time to deliver the new carousel to the festival. On his way there, Thomas rushes through Knapford Station. Emily is boarding passengers. Thomas peeps his whistle so Emily will notice how important he is.

"Good morning, Thomas!" says Emily. "Is that the new carousel?"

"I'm sorry, Emily," says Thomas. "I'm too busy to say hello."

Emily frowns. It seems Thomas thinks he is a little too important.

A short while later, Thomas arrives at the festival. Sir Topham Hatt is standing beside the tracks, looking at his pocket watch.

"Thomas, you're late!" booms Sir Topham Hatt.

"Am I?" peeps Thomas. In his excitement, he has lost track of time.

Then Sir Topham Hatt takes a closer look at the flatbeds.

"Thomas!" says Sir Topham Hatt. "A crate is missing! It must have fallen off."

Thomas hadn't even noticed. He feels very embarrassed.

"Finding the missing crate should be simple," says Sir Topham Hatt. "It should be somewhere between here and Brendam Docks."

"I'm afraid I took a longer way than that," peeps Thomas.

"Why would you take a longer way?" Sir Topham Hatt asks.

"I wanted everyone to see how important I was," puffs Thomas.

"What is most important is to be a useful engine," says Sir Topham Hatt. "Really Useful Engines show up on time and are very careful."

Sir Topham Hatt asks Thomas to look for the missing crate right away. Thomas fills up with coal at the coaling plant and chuffs back the way he came. But soon he thinks of all the places he went. Retracing his tracks might take the whole day!

Just then, Harold flies overhead, and an idea flies into Thomas' funnel!

"Hello, Harold," peeps Thomas. "I lost a crate somewhere today. Could you tell the other engines so they can help?"

"Sure thing, Thomas," says Harold. "That is a splendid idea."

Harold flies all over Sodor, telling the engines about Thomas' missing crate. Percy and Emily have already made their deliveries. They are free to help. Percy chuffs past the quarry and Tidmouth Station. He sees rabbits. He sees children flying kites.  But he does not see the missing crate.

Meanwhile, Emily rides along the coast of Sodor. She looks left, and she looks right. And she looks down too.

"Oh, dear," thinks Emily. "I hope the crate did not go too far."

Stanley drops off the Ferris wheel.  Then he chuffs to the coaling plant. He asks the workers to call Sir Topham Hatt if they see a missing crate.

"No problem, Stanley," says the foreman.

On a different part of the island, Rosie chugs through a splendid green valley, looking for the missing crate. Then she has an idea! Maybe someone found the crate and returned it to the docks.

Rosie races to the docks to ask Cranky.  But Cranky hasn't seen anything either.

"I hope the other engines are having better luck than I am," thinks Rosie.

Meanwhile, Thomas has been searching for the missing crate with Sir Topham Hatt. They have chuffed up to Bluff's Cove and stopped at many stations.

Thomas is still feeling very cross with himself for not being more careful.

Thomas is just about to give up when he hears a voice above him. It is Harold.

"Look, Thomas!" shouts Harold. "Under the bridge!"

Thomas looks. There is the missing crate!

"It must have fallen off when you were crossing the bridge," says Sir Topham Hatt.

"And now it's wet and stuck between the rocks," adds Harold.

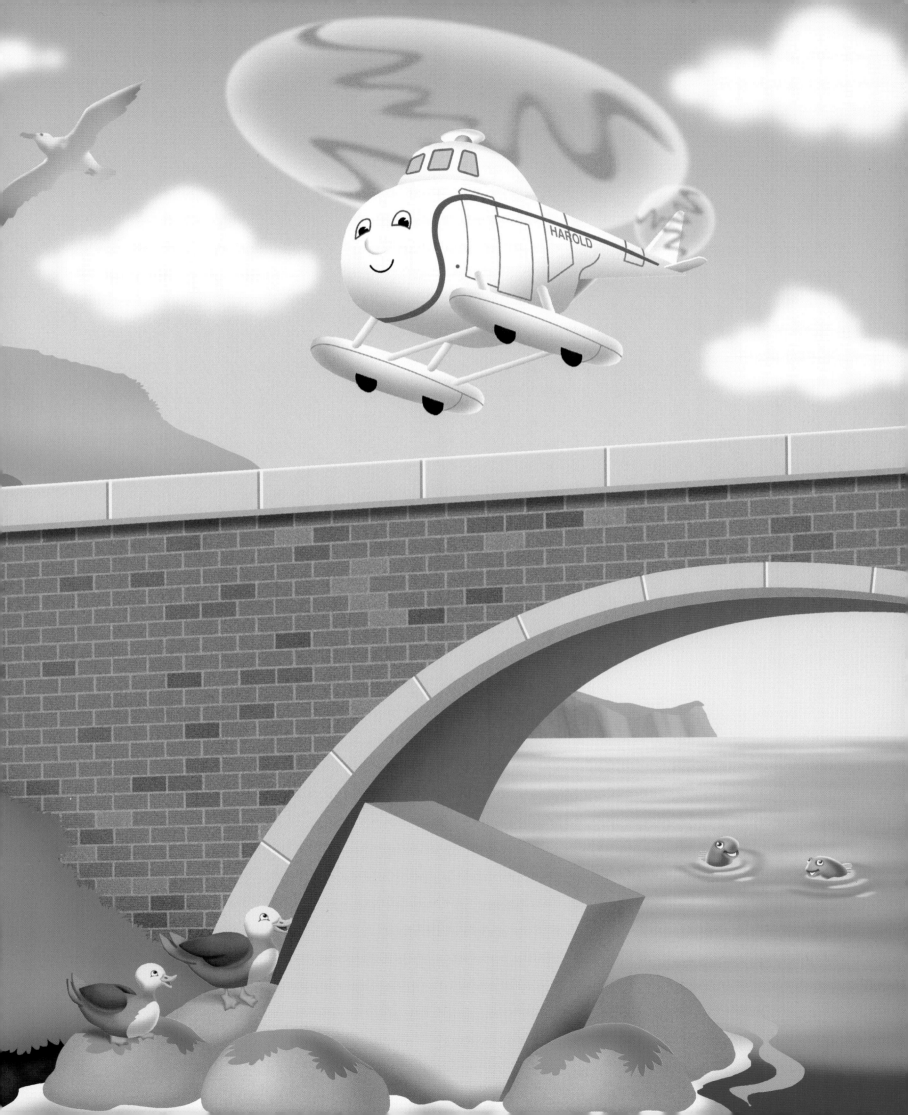

Sir Topham Hatt worries that it will be difficult to get the crate out of the water, but Thomas has an idea. Harold will ask Bulstrode to nudge the crate out of the rocks. Harold will lift the crate onto Thomas' flatbed. Sir Topham Hatt will secure the crate and tighten the chains.

"That is a splendid idea, Thomas!" exclaims Sir Topham Hatt.

A short time later, the missing crate is back on the flatbed. Thomas' plan worked! Thomas heads off to the festival.

"This time I will be very careful, Sir Topham Hatt," he promises.

BULSTRODE

When Thomas and Sir Topham Hatt arrive with the missing crate, the people of Sodor cheer, the children loudest of all. The workers take off the chains, and Madge helps move the crate from the tracks. Together, the workers assemble the carousel, piece by piece.

Finally, the new carousel is complete!

The other engines show up just in time to see Sir Topham Hatt take the first official ride.

Afterwards, Sir Topham Hatt walks over to Thomas.

"You were a Really Useful Engine today, Thomas," says Sir Topham Hatt. "Really Useful Engines learn from their mistakes."

"*All* of us were Really Useful Engines today," says Thomas.

As the sun dips over the horizon, Thomas and his friends peep their whistles. The fireworks display begins. This is the best Sodor Summer Festival yet!